South Lanarkshire Libraries

This book is to be returned on or before
the last date stamped below or may be
renewed by telephone or online.

SOUTH LANARKSHIRE
Leisure & Culture
ww.library.southlanarkshire.gov.uk

Delivering services for South Lanarkshire

Also by Marcus Sedgwick
for older readers

The Raven Mysteries

Elf Girl and Raven Boy

Visit Marcus Sedgwick's website at –
www.marcussedgwick.com

DREAD DESERT

ELF GIRL and RAVEN BOY

MARCUS SEDGWICK

Illustrated by Pete Williamson

Orion
Children's Books

First published in Great Britain in 2013
by Orion Children's Books
a division of the Orion Publishing Group Ltd
Orion House
5 Upper St Martin's Lane
London WC2H 9EA
An Hachette UK Company

1 3 5 7 9 10 8 6 4 2

Copyright © Marcus Sedgwick 2013
Illustrations copyright © Pete Williamson 2013
Inside design by www.hereandnowdesign.com

A catalogue record for this book is available from the British
Library.

ISBN 978 1 4440 0526 4

Printed in Great Britain by CPI Group (UK) Ltd,
Croydon, CR0 4YY

www.orionbooks.co.uk

Two

It's true that Elf Girl has a quick temper, but she also has a big heart and is very fond of Raven Boy, though she'd probably never admit it.

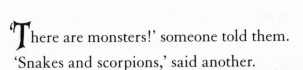

'There are monsters!' someone told them.

'Snakes and scorpions,' said another.

'Sandstorms and all sorts of other dangers,' said a third person, reading from a leaflet called 'Why you should never go to Dread Desert, ever.'

'Raven Boy,' said Elf Girl. 'I am severely not happy about this one.'

'Come on,' said Raven Boy, sounding

scared and feeling even worse, 'how bad can it be? We faced Fright Forest and lived to tell the tale. Even those trolls couldn't catch us.'

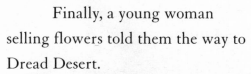

'They haven't stopped trying yet, though, have they?' Elf Girl pointed out, and Raven Boy went quiet.

Finally, a young woman selling flowers told them the way to Dread Desert.

'It's very easy. All you do is walk inland. That way, east. Whichever way you go, you'll be in Dread Desert.'

'But we have to find the centre of it,' explained Raven Boy.

'Why would you want to do that?' asked the flower-seller.

'We just do,' said Elf Girl, quietly.

'That's a bit harder. I don't think anyone knows where the centre is. It moves, you see?'

'Moves?' cried Elf Girl and Raven Boy together.

'Yes, the desert's always moving, and

always growing, so the centre of it doesn't stay in one place. That's what they say, anyway.'

Elf Girl swallowed hard.

'Come on, Raven Boy,' she said. 'Let's go.'

'Go?' wailed Raven Boy. 'Go where? We don't even know which way to go.'

'Yes, we do,' said Elf Girl. 'We go that way. East. And we'll find the centre of the desert somehow.'

Raven Boy looked very unhappy and Rat went and hid in his pocket, refusing to come out.

'Well,' Raven Boy said, 'if we're going to march into the desert, we ought to take some supplies with us.'

'Supplies?' asked Elf Girl. 'Sort of like third breakfast, you mean?'

A dreamy look came over Raven Boy's face.

'Third breakfast,' he whispered, almost to himself. 'Third breakfast?'

He smiled at Elf Girl.

'You're really quite clever,' he said, and so, with Raven Boy muttering, 'Who'd have thought it?' and 'Well I never!' to himself, they went to find a third breakfast, one that they could easily carry into the desert.

By tea-time Waterspout was far behind them, long vanished over the horizon. For most of the day they'd walked through a dry and dusty land, with scrubby grass and not a single tree to be seen.

Finally, the sun started to set behind them and, as it sank, they reached the edge of the sand. Sand as far as the eye could see, stretching off into the distance over rolling dunes, with not so much as a single blade of grass to show that anything was alive out there.

'Dread Desert!' wailed Raven Boy. He pulled a piece of paper from his pocket.

'"Alongside a wide variety of the world's deadliest creatures . . ."' he began, but Elf Girl snatched the paper from him.

It was the leaflet called 'Why you should never go to Dread Desert, ever'.

'What did you bring that for?' she asked.

'I thought it might be a good idea,' Raven Boy said.

'You were wrong,' said Elf Girl. She tore the leaflet up into pieces, and threw them on the ground.

'Hey!' said Raven Boy. 'You mustn't do that!'

'What?'

'Drop litter!' said Raven Boy firmly. He began to pick up the pieces of paper. 'You should never leave a mess anywhere. Even this place must be home to something!'

Elf Girl looked around.

'Like what?' she asked. 'Look at it! There's nothing here! Nothing!'

'Apart from all the things listed in this!' said Raven Boy, clutching the torn pieces of the leaflet.

Elf Girl suddenly stared at Raven Boy.

'I didn't know you could read,' she said.

Raven Boy stood up, blinking.

'Nor did I,' he said. 'Fancy that.'

'Maybe you learned a long time ago. When you were little?'

Raven Boy blinked some more.

'Maybe your parents taught you. So long ago that you can't remember.'

Raven Boy shook his head.

'I don't know,' he said. 'I just don't know.'

'Well, it's a jolly good thing you can read. It's very useful, you know. And educational.'

'Yes,' agreed Raven Boy, looking cross and waving the paper at Elf Girl. 'You could, for example, teach yourself about the dangers of the desert from a helpful leaflet. Or at least you could have done if someone hadn't torn it up!'

Elf Girl was silent.

The sun set, and they sat down.

'There's no point going further tonight,' Elf Girl said. 'We'll wait until morning.'

'We may as well have a bedtime snack,' said Raven Boy, and Elf Girl laughed.

'Yes,' she said, 'and I bet, by ten o'clock tomorrow morning we'll have found the centre of the desert and be on our way home with the Tears of the Moon and the Singing Sword.'

THREE

One wintertime, Rat got snowed into his burrow in the forest. It took him two weeks to dig his way out, but still he prefers the forest to the dry desert.

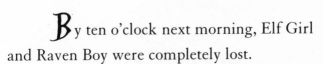

By ten o'clock next morning, Elf Girl and Raven Boy were completely lost.

Not only that, but they had finished all their food and only had a little bit of water left.

'Lost!' cheeped Raven Boy.

They trudged on and on through the sand, and as the morning passed, the sun got higher and higher in the sky and as it did, it got hotter and hotter.

Raven Boy did a very rare thing; he took off his coat to cool down. As the sun got ever hotter, he and Elf Girl used the coat as a shade. They stretched it over Elf Girl's bow and held it above their heads till their arms got too tired, and they had to rest.

The sand was so hot it hurt to sit on, sweat was pouring down their faces, and Rat had long ago burrowed into Raven Boy's trouser pocket.

'Elf Girl,' panted Raven Boy, 'I don't think we're going to make it.'

'Of course we are!' puffed Elf Girl, pulling a sweaty strand of hair out of her eyes.

'We are?' said Raven Boy. 'We don't even know where we're going! We're completely lost!'

'Yes,' said Elf Girl, nodding weakly, 'but that's a good thing.'

'It is?'

'Absolutely.'

'Because?'

'Because,' said Elf Girl, as if she was speaking to a dim rabbit, 'because we don't know where we're trying to get to. And if we don't know where we're trying to get to, then we'd have to be lost to get there, wouldn't we?'

Raven Boy didn't say anything for a minute, but stared up into the sky, blinking.

Then he said, 'My head hurts.'

'Oh, Raven Boy,' Elf Girl snapped, 'just trust me. Everything's going to be fine. Come on, rest time's over. Time to get walking again.'

They set off once more, with the hot sun beating down and their feet sinking into the soft sand, which made walking even slower. Up and down the dunes they went, and in every direction there was nothing to be seen but the sand.

They finished their water, and Raven Boy even allowed Elf Girl to leave the empty stone bottle behind in the sand, now that it was no use to them.

They walked, and they walked, and their faces started to burn, even though they held Raven Boy's coat over their heads when they could, and lay under it every time they stopped to rest.

Rat was sulking, and when he did make a brief appearance to squeak abuse at them for bringing him into Dread Desert, he looked very bedraggled indeed.

He gave one mighty last squeak and then lay on the sand, panting, and waving his paws in the air.

'He says it's not fair. He says I can take my coat off, but he can't. And his is made of fur too.'

'Poor Rat,' said Elf Girl. 'Why doesn't he sit on your shoulder in the shade of your coat while we walk? The breeze will cool him off.'

So that's what they did, and Rat looked happier for a while until, some time later, he shrieked in alarm.

'What?' cried Elf Girl.

'He says we're back where we started!' wailed Raven Boy.

'We can't be!'

'Yes, we are! Look!'

It was true. They had caught up with their own footsteps.

'Maybe they're someone else's footprints,' said Elf Girl, hopefully, but then they saw their empty water bottle, and they knew it was true.

'Oh no!' cried Raven Boy. 'We've been walking in circles! We're completely lost!'

'Good!' declared Elf Girl. 'Because . . .'

'Don't start that again,' said Raven Boy. 'My head hurts enough as it is.'

They walked, and they walked, and still the sun beat down, and finally they did see other signs of life.

There were strange marks in the sand, here and there, which they guessed were made by snakes, and scorpions, and others of the world's most dangerous creatures.

'If only we saw one of them,' said Raven Boy, weakly, 'I could ask which way the centre of the desert is.'

'Are you sure?' asked Elf Girl. 'I mean, speaking to cuddly badgers is one thing, but are you sure you'd get a polite reply out of a scorpion?'

'Maybe,' said Raven Boy. 'I don't actually know what a scorpion is.'

'Well,' explained Elf Girl, 'it's one of the world's most . . .'

'Yes, thank you. I got that much,' said Raven Boy. 'Come on. Time to get lost some more.'

So they walked on and the sun got hotter and they got grumpier and more tired and their clothes were soaked through with sweat, and they clambered up sand dunes on their hands and knees, and then rolled down the other side, which should have been fun, but wasn't.

By now their shoes were full of sand, and they had to stop every five minutes to empty them out, but somehow there always seemed to be some left between their toes.

As they walked it seemed that the landscape was changing around them, almost as if the dunes were moving. All in all it was no wonder they were lost.

And then, just when things were looking their worst, Raven Boy suddenly gave a huge whoop of joy.

'Hey! Look!'

Elf Girl could barely see – her eyes were hidden behind her tangled sweaty hair – but as she made a gap to look through, she saw what Raven Boy had seen.

'Hey! A lake!'

There, a short way ahead, they could see a beautiful shimmering lake, cool and inviting.

'Come on!' they both screamed, and

summoning what energy they could, they ran towards it, both eager to be the first to dive in.

They ran fast, and then, just as they jumped, the water disappeared from right under them, vanishing into thin air.

'What?' roared Elf Girl, looking so cross her ears might have caught fire.

Raven Boy didn't say anything; he'd decided to jump head first, and was stuck in the sand with only his legs visible, pointing at the sky.

They wiggled a bit, until Elf Girl sighed and pulled him out.

'Puh-fuff,' said Raven Boy, spitting sand out of his mouth. 'What happened?'

Elf Girl glared.

'Stupid desert. It tricked us. One moment there was a nice pool of water, the next . . .'

'It just disappeared,' Raven Boy said. 'Stupid desert.'

Rat squeaked.

'He said . . .' began Raven Boy.

'Yes,' said Elf Girl. 'I got it. Stupid desert.'

'Yes,' said Raven Boy, 'only he used a worse word than stupid.'

Elf Girl stood up.

'Raven Boy,' she said. 'I've made a decision.'

'You have?' said Raven Boy, standing up, looking a bit happier now that Elf Girl seemed to have some kind of plan that would help them.

'Yes,' said Elf Girl. 'I've decided that we

are going to die a horrible slow death in this stupid desert and so we may as well just lie down and give up.'

'Oh,' said Raven Boy.

'Oh?' said Elf Girl. 'Is that all you've got to say?'

'Well, I have to admit I'm a bit . . . disappointed about that.'

'You know, Raven Boy, so am I. I was very much hoping to save the Sword of the Moon and the Singing Tears and . . .'

'Are you feeling all right?' asked Raven Boy. 'This heat, you know, it can . . .'

And with that Elf Girl fainted in the sand and lay still.

FOUR

Raven Boy doesn't know lots of things about who he is, or who his parents were. All he can remember is living in the forest, since he was small.

Raven Boy panicked.

'Elf Girl! Wake up!' he cried. 'I know it's hot and horrible and everything. But you have to wake up! You can't leave me!'

He tried everything.

He wafted air over her face, and tugged her arms. He pulled her hair out of her eyes and even took her boots off and tickled her toes, which strangely were as pointy as the boots she wore.

Nothing worked, and Raven Boy was concentrating so hard on trying to make Elf Girl wake up that he didn't notice a huge shadow blot out the sun behind him.

As he tried blowing up Elf Girl's nose, however, he suddenly realised the sun wasn't as fierce as it had been.

'Elf Girl!' he cried again, 'Wake up! The sun's gone in.'

Elf Girl opened one eye sleepily. She sat up a fraction.

'Camel,' she said, and collapsed in the sand again.

'What?' asked Raven Boy, and then there was a noisy snorting sound behind him, and he turned and shrieked, as he saw a giant beast looming over them.

Rat squeaked and hid under Raven Boy's coat. Raven Boy slowly began to realise that the big creature wasn't trying to kill him, or eat him, or for that matter even trying to nibble him, though it had a set of teeth that could have done some pretty high-quality chewing, if need be.

It had a hump on its back, and stood on four legs. Its feet were the size of large dinner plates, and it had a short tail like a brush that seemed to attract a lot of flies.

'Are you . . . ?' asked Raven Boy. 'Are you a scorpion?'

The beast snorted and Elf Girl groaned.

She sat up, blinking.

'Raven Boy, you are a very ignorant bird sometimes. This is a camel.'

The camel snorted.

'A camel?' echoed Raven Boy. 'Not a scorpion?'

'A camel,' said Elf Girl. 'This is definitely a camel.'

'And what are camels like?'

'They're big on being grumpy,' said Elf Girl, 'and they have unpleasant habits.'

'Such as?'

'Such as spitting a lot. And did I mention being grumpy? But it's very good news for us, because you can ask it for a ride.'

'I can?' asked Raven Boy.

Nervously he stood a tiny bit closer to the camel.

'It has a label on it,' he said, noticing a small tag tied round the beast's neck. 'It says "Property of T.T." I wonder who that is . . .'

'Well, why don't you ask it? You're always telling me you can speak to animals.'

'Not speak, as such. I just understand them, and they . . .'

'They understand you. Yes, you told me. However it works, camels give rides, and so you can ask him to take us to the centre of the desert and out again. Yes?'

Raven Boy blinked. He looked at the

camel. The camel looked down at him with one eye, looking, well, there is no other word for it but grumpy.

'Err, Camel,' began Raven Boy. 'Mr Camel, even. Erm, could we, I mean, perhaps you could . . . ? That is to say . . .'

'Oh, for goodness' sake!' cried Elf Girl.

'Don't rush me!' said Raven Boy, and he stood up and began whispering into the camel's ear. When he'd finished, Raven Boy stepped back and the camel took one look at them both and then weed on the sand.

'He says no,' said Raven Boy.

'He did?'

'In fact, he didn't say anything at all.
He just . . .'

'Yes, I saw what he did, thank you very
much,' said Elf Girl, wrinkling her nose. 'But
that's too bad, because we need him. If he
doesn't take us for a ride, I've a good mind just
to lie down again and . . .'

'No!' cried Raven Boy. 'I'll try again.'

'Good bird,' said Elf Girl. 'Wait! I have
an idea! Maybe he doesn't speak the same way
you do. Maybe we just need to show him what
we want. Let's climb up on his back and then
maybe he'll get the idea.'

Raven Boy wasn't too sure about that,
but Elf Girl threatened to faint again, so they
climbed up onto the camel's back.

Now, as has been pointed out before,
Raven Boy is extremely good at climbing. Rat
is not too bad at all, and Elf Girl is completely
rubbish. So, very soon, Rat and Raven Boy were
on the camel's back, where there was a sort

of seat made out of a rug and some ropes and pieces of wood, looking down at Elf Girl who was hopping about in the sand, getting madder and madder by the second.

Her face was already sunburned, but Raven Boy was pretty sure the tips of her ears were redder than they'd been five minutes before, and he knew that was a bad sign.

'Here,' said Raven Boy, holding on to the seat and lowering a hand towards his pointy friend, 'if you jump a bit I'll grab you and try and pull you up, and . . .'

Then he stopped talking because he was screaming instead.

'What?' squealed Elf Girl, who turned round to see what he was looking at. All she could see was desert.

Raven Boy was still screaming, and began frantically trying to pull Elf Girl on board the camel.

'T-t-trolls!' screamed Raven Boy. 'Trolls! They're back!'

Now even Elf Girl could see them, as they lumbered over a sand dune, heading right for them.

'They must have followed our tracks!' Raven Boy cried. '**E**EP!'

'Quick! Pull me up!'

And this time, Elf Girl managed to scramble onto the camel with Raven Boy's help.

'Quick!' she cried. 'Get it moving!'

'I'm trying!' wailed Raven Boy.

'They're getting close!'

'I'm doing my best.'

'How do you drive a camel?' asked Elf Girl.

'I don't know!' screamed Raven Boy.

The trolls were now stomping up the slope towards them, roaring:

'Gotcha!'

and

'Suppertime!'

and

'Horse for pudding!'

'It's a camel, you idiot!'

'All right, camel for pudding then!'

'**E**EEEEEP!' cried Raven Boy and Elf Girl, who were kicking the camel and slapping its sides, and then Rat ran towards the camel's back end, and sank his two sharp front teeth as deep as he could manage into its bottom.

The effect was incredible.

They could not have accelerated faster if they had been fixed to a firework. The camel shot off across the sand with Raven Boy, Elf Girl and Rat clinging on for dear life.

The camel did not stop, and showed no sign of stopping for a long time and, when it finally did, it was dark, and they rolled off its back and lay looking up into the night sky, where a million million stars were twinkling.

'Raven Boy,' said Elf Girl, quietly.

'Yes, Elf Girl?'

'My bottom hurts.'

'So does mine,' said Raven Boy. 'Nasty camel. Tomorrow we'll see if we can get him to go a bit more slowly.'

'Do you think the trolls are far enough away?'

'Yes, I'm sure of it,' said Raven Boy. 'Thanks to Rat.'

Rat squeaked happily and, despite their sore behinds, they all went to sleep smiling.

FIVE

Raven Boy will talk to any animal that talks back, but he likes chatting to bunnies best of all. They have a silly sense of humour that always makes him giggle.

As it turned out, the camel didn't go more slowly next day, because when they woke up, it had gone.

'You should have tied it to something,' said Elf Girl.

'Oh yes, I should have tied it to something!' said Raven Boy. 'Something like what? Look!'

They were in the middle of the wide,

wide desert, and there was nothing but sand to be seen in every direction.

'Maybe you could have chatted to it a bit more, and asked it to stay.'

'If you remember, it wasn't a very chatty camel. Let's just say we're better off without it and leave it at that. At least our bottoms won't get so sore today.'

Elf Girl looked worried, and Raven Boy knew why. Without anything to eat and no water to drink, they'd be lucky if they lasted another day in Dread Desert.

'Listen,' said Raven Boy. 'That camel must have come from somewhere. He had that name tag on him, T.T., so he has an owner. He probably ran away.'

'Or was sent packing for being too grumpy.'

'Either way, it must mean someone is out here somewhere, so we just have to go on and find them before . . .'

But he didn't finish his sentence because he didn't like the way it was going to end.

If their day started badly with the camel going missing, it soon got worse.

They walked on and on and still saw nothing but sand and sky, sand and sky. And sun. There was always a big hot sun shining down on them, making everything harder than it should have been, and sand piling up in their shoes every five minutes, sand that seemed to shift and move every time they weren't looking.

'Just think,' said Elf Girl. 'At least when they bury us, we'll have really nice suntans.'

Raven Boy chuckled, but only to be polite. Secretly he was worrying a lot, and doubted very much that anyone would bury them. They'd lie in the sand for a thousand years before anyone found them, and by then they'd be three sets of shiny, white bones; two large and one tiny.

They'd wandered away from the sand dunes now and were in a flatter piece of desert, though still there was nothing to be seen but sand. And then without warning, a figure rose out of the ground: a giant, made of sand.

It roared, and began to run towards them.

'EEEP!' cried Raven Boy. 'Elf Girl! Do something. Do something with your bow! Shoot it, even!'

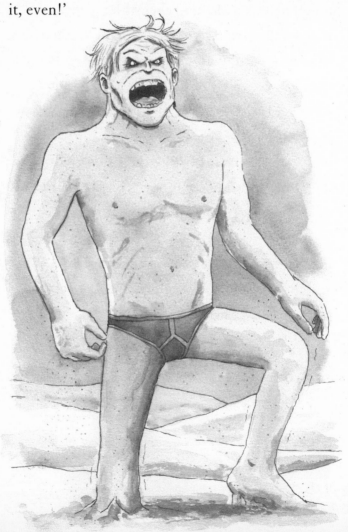

Elf Girl didn't reply because she was too busy pulling her magic bow out from Raven Boy's coat and aiming it at the sand giant.

It was enormous. It towered over them, hiding the sun even more effectively than the camel had. It had a nasty scowl on its face and roared again as it approached, sand flying from its mouth. Although they'd never seen such a creature before, it reminded Raven Boy of something.

'Quickly!' Raven Boy yelled, but Elf Girl was concentrating, because the trouble with her magic bow was that you never knew what it was going to do.

Raven Boy saw the arrow-shaped birth-mark on her arm start to glow as it always did, and the invisible bowstring suddenly became visible, shining brightly.

Elf Girl fired and Raven Boy cheered, because, for the first time ever, a real arrow flew from the bow and hurtled towards the sand giant.

'Yay!' cheered Raven Boy, but then he howled as Elf Girl's arrow missed the monster.

There was time for one more try, and

then it would be on them.

Elf Girl fired again, and another real arrow shot from the bow.

This time it headed straight for the beast, and Raven Boy cheered again, but they both watched in horror as the arrow not only hit it, but went straight through it, leaving it completely unharmed.

'No!' they screamed, and the sand giant reached down two massive hands and picked them both up into the air.

'Eeeep!' they screeched as it waved them around, high above the desert, and then opened its mouth, and crammed them inside, Elf Girl first, Raven Boy with Rat in his pocket second.

Everything turned into a sandy mess. They couldn't see and they couldn't breathe, but they felt themselves falling, falling, falling. They landed with a bump.

They both passed out, and when they woke, they were surrounded not by sand giants, but a circle of Sandmen and Sandwomen.

'So!' one of the Sandmen shouted. 'You'd come into our desert! Come here to steal!'

'Steal what?' asked Elf Girl. 'Your sand?'

'This is our desert!' cried the Sandman. 'You have no right to be here!'

Raven Boy looked at Elf Girl.

'Don't you recognise them?' he asked. 'Remember Mervin? On the island?'

'Raven Boy, you're right!' cried Elf Girl.

'I usually am,' said Raven Boy, winking.

'No, you're not,' said Elf Girl, 'And that's my line, anyway.'

Meanwhile, the Sandman had stopped dead.

'Did you say Mervin?' he asked.

'Yes, Mervin. We met him on an island in the Scream Sea. He's one of you, isn't he?'

The Sandman frowned.

'He was, you know, but he ran away. Haven't seen him in ages.'

He turned to his friends.

'They've seen Mervin!' he called, and they all came close and began fussing around and asking lots of questions.

'Where is he?'

'Is he all right?'

'Where did you see him?'

'Did he send you here?'

'Is he eating properly?'

'Why did he run away, anyway?' someone asked.

'He mentioned something about peace and quiet,' Raven Boy said.

'Peace and quiet?' said another. 'It's perfectly peaceful out here in the desert. Whatever could he mean?'

Elf Girl and Raven Boy looked at each other, and their eyebrows raised, because they'd only just met the Sandpeople, and already their ears were ringing from all the questions.

'Now, then, look at the state of you two . . . or three! Who's this little fellow, anyway? You probably want something to drink, don't you? I expect we can magic something up for you. Wouldn't that be nice? You'd like that, wouldn't you? You like sandwiches, I hope.'

They went on, and on, and on, chattering until Raven Boy thought his ears might fall off.

SIX

Elf Girl's bow has been in her family for years and years, passed down from mother to daughter. She'd love to know how it works properly.

The problem with Sandpeople was . . .

Actually, Raven Boy decided, there were two problems with Sandpeople. First of all, they were made of sand.

Now, that might sound pretty obvious, but it made life very difficult for anyone not made of sand. Anyone, in this case, being Elf Girl, and Raven Boy and Rat, because when they got to the Sandpeople's village, it was made entirely of sand.

In fact, it was very hard at first to even tell they were in the village, because it looked just like another empty patch of desert to Raven Boy.

He and Elf Girl soon learned that Sandpeople are very strange indeed. Not only are they made of the same stuff that beaches are, but so is everything they own and everything they eat. For example, if they fancied a nice little sit-down, some sand would rise out of the desert and become a chair, and if they got a bit sleepy, they could even make a comfy bed of sand to lie on. Usually, however, when the Sandpeople went to sleep, they just dissolved into the desert and seemed to have disappeared.

They could form themselves together to make something really big, like when they'd made the scary sand giant that had captured Elf Girl and Raven Boy.

And then there was their food. Because all that the Sandpeople ate was sand, and they seemed to eat for something to do, rather than because they actually needed any sandwiches – which were actually made of sand.

The second problem was that they never shut up. Not for one minute. They talked all the time, hardly listening to what anyone else was saying, and after half an hour, Raven Boy was ready to scream.

Elf Girl, on the other hand, was ready to faint

again, with hunger.

'Please,' she said when she managed to get a word in between the Sandpeople's conversations. 'Please. Could you make us some food? Some food not made of sand?'

'Not made of sand?' said the nearest Sandman. 'Why would you want food not made of sand?'

'Because we can't eat sand,' Elf Girl explained, politely. 'And when we were on the island with Mervin, he made us lots of lovely things to eat, and none of them were made of sand.'

'Really?' said the Sandman. 'Fancy that. He always was a clever one.'

'You can make normal food, can't you?' asked Raven Boy, looking worried.

The Sandman shrugged.

'Sand is normal,' he said. 'Sorry.'

Raven Boy clutched his rumbling tummy and groaned.

SEVEN

Dread Desert might sound like a scary place, but it's a picnic compared with what lies ahead for Raven Boy and Elf Girl.

By next morning, Raven Boy and Elf Girl were fit to burst. They had had very little sleep, listening to the Sandpeople chattering all night long. Rat looked fed up, and though he'd tried blocking his ears with his tail, he could only block one of them at a time, and that made him restless, as he'd kept switching ears all night.

Finally, one of the Sandpeople actually stopped talking long enough for Raven Boy to ask them a question.

'You don't know where the centre of the desert is, do you?'

The Sandman rubbed his sandy face.

'No idea,' he said. 'But why would you want to go there, anyway?'

'Because we have to. We've been told that the Tears of the Moon and the Singing Sword can be found there.'

'Oh, and what are they?'

Elf Girl and Raven Boy looked embarrassed.

'We don't know,' said Elf Girl.

'So why do you want these things, if you don't know what they are?' asked the Sandman.

'The Singing Sword is a sword that sings!' cried Raven Boy. 'We know that much.'

'Whatever they are,' said Elf Girl, 'we need them to fight the Goblin King.'

Finally, all the Sandpeople stopped talking. For a long time. What they did was whisper instead and once or twice Elf Girl and Raven Boy heard them mutter the name of their deadly enemy.

'You know about the Goblin King?' asked Elf Girl.

'Oh yes,' said the Sandman, 'we know about the Goblin King, we know all about him. He's the reason for this desert. He's the reason we're here, he's the reason that Sandpeople are Sandpeople.'

Then the Sandman told them a long, sad story, all about how the Goblin King was responsible for Dread Desert.

'You see,' the Sandman said, 'once upon a time, this wasn't a desert at all. It was a huge forest.'

'A forest!' cried Raven Boy. 'A forest with trees?'

'That's the usual thing, isn't it,' muttered Elf Girl, but the Sandman was going on with his story.

'You see, we had a nice forest here, and

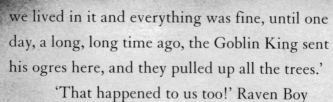

we lived in it and everything was fine, until one day, a long, long time ago, the Goblin King sent his ogres here, and they pulled up all the trees.'

'That happened to us too!' Raven Boy exclaimed. 'Well, he tried to, at least.'

But the Sandman wasn't listening.

'And once all the trees were gone,' he said, 'the animals disappeared, and even the

grass was blown away, and over the years it turned into this terrible desert. We were lucky, because we found a magician who turned us into Sandpeople, and that's how we've been ever since!'

Raven Boy and Elf Girl looked at each other, their eyes wide.

'So that's what will happen
to the rest of the world if we don't stop
the Goblin King!' cried Raven Boy.

Elf Girl nodded, and turned to the
Sandman who'd told them the story.

'That's why we have to stop the Goblin
King. That's why we need the Tears of the
Moon and the Singing Sword. That's why we
have to find the centre of Dread Desert.'

'Oh!' cried the Sandpeople. 'No! Far too
dangerous!'

'You'll never succeed! Look at us! We
got turned into sand!'

'No one knows where the centre of the
desert is.'

'No one!'

'No, no one. No one except . . .'

'Except?' asked Raven Boy, interrupting.
'Except who?'

'There is one person who might . . .'

'Who?' said Elf Girl. 'You have to tell us!'

'Well, if you insist on getting yourself
killed, you might try and find Jean.'

'Jean? Who's Jean?'

'She's a magical being, and very wise. She's the one who made us into sand. She knows everything. She might be able to help you. But she lives a long way from here in a secret cave in the northern desert. You'd die of thirst long before you found her.'

'Not if you told us where to go, and gave us some bottles of water,' said Raven Boy. 'You have to. You have to help us stop the Goblin King before the whole world is like this!'

The Sandpeople all began muttering to each other, for quite some time, but finally they agreed.

'Very well,' one of them said. 'We'll find you some water. And some nice parasols to keep the sun off. What colour would you like?'

'You'll really help us?' asked Raven Boy.

'Yes, we'll show you which way to go, you'll just have to do your best not to get lost.'

'We promise,' said Elf Girl. 'Though it's very hard. The desert is very strange. We thought we saw a pool of water and it just vanished when we went to get it.'

The Sandpeople laughed.

'It wasn't funny!' said Elf Girl, and her ears started turning pink.

'It's called a mirage,' said one of the Sandwomen, chuckling. 'It happens sometimes when you're lost in the desert. You think you see something that isn't really there. You're not the first people to be caught out.'

Raven Boy and Elf Girl looked at each other, their eyes gaping.

'This place is crazy,' said Raven Boy, and Elf Girl nodded.

'The sooner we get to magical Jean and get out of here, the better,' Elf Girl said.

'Elf Girl,' said Raven Boy, 'you're right.'

And Elf Girl was so overcome with it all, she didn't even have the heart to say, 'I always am.'

'So how do we find Jean?' asked Raven Boy.

'Her cave is secret, but there are some hills in the northern desert and that's where it is. But when you find it, you can't get in without saying the secret word.'

'Which is?' asked Elf Girl.

'If we knew that, it wouldn't be a secret, would it?'

That was hard to argue with, and Raven Boy and Elf Girl decided that all they could do was think of all the things the secret word could be, and then try them all out once they found the cave.

It seemed like a very bad plan indeed, because it was.

EIGHT

No one knows much about the Goblin King. Only that he's very mean and very greedy and wants to take over the world.

It seemed a very silly thing to do; to walk into the northern desert and find the secret cave where Jean lived. And sure enough, by the middle of the day after they'd left the sand village, Raven Boy and Elf Girl were lost and though they had nice pink parasols to keep the sun off, they were hot, grumpy and very, very fed up.

They were running out of water again.

'Raven Boy,' wailed Elf Girl, 'I really hate the desert.'

Raven Boy was so tired he could barely answer, but he did manage a sigh.

'Yes,' he said. 'And just think, if we don't stop the Goblin King, the whole world will become like this.'

'I hate the Goblin King too,' Elf Girl muttered.

Raven Boy didn't answer, but kept plodding along through the hot sand, step after step.

The Sandpeople had shown them which way north was, and yet it was hard to be sure they were still going the right way.

'What a place!' Raven Boy moaned. 'There's nothing here! Nothing but sand, nowhere to stop, nowhere to hide from the sun.'

'Yes, there is!' cried Elf Girl suddenly. 'Look!'

She pointed into the distance, where there was a small group of trees, standing all alone by some low sand hills.

'Look!'

'Yay!' Raven Boy said, cheering up, 'At least we can have a rest in the shade of the trees. It will be almost like home. Come on!'

So they ran to the trees, as fast as the sinking sand would let them run, and then, just as they made it, the trees vanished.

Pff! Gone. Vanished into thin air.

'Oh! Oh no!' groaned Elf Girl. 'Another of those stupid mirage things!'

'I really, really hate the desert,' said Raven Boy. 'I hate it!'

And, rather wistfully, he thought of
his forest home, with its lovely tall trees that
swayed in the breeze, of the little streams that
wound their way here and there between the
tree trunks, and of all the small cuddly animals
he'd chat to as he went about collecting something
nice to eat for breakfast. So different from this
awful hot place!

'We're never going to find Jean!' Raven
Boy said.

'And even if we do, we haven't even
started trying to guess what the secret password
could be.'

'Password? Like Open Sesame, you mean?'

'Yes, and Abracadabra,' said Elf Girl.

'That's a good one!' cried Raven Boy.
'How about Alakazam?'

'Not bad,' nodded Elf Girl.

'Monkey-moo!'

'That's silly.'

'Is not. You do better then.'

'I will. Trunkety-trunk!'

Raven Boy laughed.

'Shimaloo-shimalee!' he said.

Elf Girl giggled.

'Squonk.'

'I don't think it's Squonk,' said Raven Boy. 'How about Mobie-spalobie?'

'I don't think it's that either,' said Elf Girl, and she giggled some more.

Then she stopped giggling and so did Raven Boy.

'Face it,' she said. 'Even if we find this place, we're never going to guess the secret word.'

Raven Boy blinked and Rat gave a mournful squeak.

'Don't tell me,' said Elf Girl. 'He's as fed up as we are.'

Raven Boy nodded.

'Yes, he is. But he also wondered if the secret word might be Jean.'

'Jean?' spluttered Elf Girl, a little unkindly. 'Jean? It's not going to be her name, is it?'

'It could be,' said Raven Boy, trying to avoid Rat's feelings being hurt. 'Or something like it. Like Jeanie-weenie. Or Weenie-Jeanie.'

'Weenie-Jeanie?' cried Elf Girl, snorting rudely. 'Don't be . . .'

She didn't finish what she was saying, because there was a terrific rumbling sound, and the ground shook under their feet.

The sand began to swirl, and then a huge pointed rock pushed itself into the air. The earth stopped shaking, the sand settled, and all three of them stared at the rock.

In its centre was a small hole, just like the doorway to a cave, because that was what it was.

'Well . . .' whispered Raven Boy.

'Holy Monkeys!' cried Elf Girl. 'We did it!'

'Rat did it!' laughed Raven Boy.

They stared at the cave mouth.

'It looks dark in there,' said Raven Boy. 'You know, scary and dark.'

'Raven Boy,' said Elf Girl, firmly, 'you know we have to go in there. And anyway, it will be cool. Wouldn't you rather be out of the hot sun?'

Raven Boy stared at the scary-looking cave.

'I could stay out here and work on my tan,' he said.

Elf Girl glared at him, and her ears turned pink, but not pink enough to make

Raven Boy think he'd rather go into the cave
than stay outside.

'Raven Boy! You know we have to! We
have to find this Jean and get her to help us.
Now stop being such a scaredy-bird and let's get
on with it.'

Raven Boy blinked.

'Okay,' he said, in a small and frightened
voice. 'Come on then. Rat, you'd better get in
my pocket. We don't want anyone stepping on
you in the dark.'

Holding hands, Raven Boy and Elf Girl tip-toed into the cave.

It was strange, because inside it wasn't as dark as they'd been expecting. They kept holding hands anyway, though, just in case, but as they walked in further and further, they could still see easily, though the doorway was far behind them now.

'Where's the light coming from?' Raven Boy whispered.

'All around us,' Elf Girl whispered back. 'Look!'

It was true. The rock walls of the cave seemed to glow with a kind of light that came from inside them, like magic.

But if it was helpful having the light to see by, it was also scary, because it showed them that the floor of the cave was covered in bones. Lots and lots of bones. They looked very much like they might have belonged to people, once upon a time.

'Are those . . . ?' began Raven Boy.

'No, I'm sure they're not. They're probably animal bones.'

Rat squeaked unhappily.

'Jean?' called Elf Girl.

'Shh!' hushed Raven Boy. 'She might hear you!'

'That's what we want her to do, silly bird,' said Elf Girl. 'Stop being so scared. Come on, help me call out for her.'

'No need,' said Raven Boy.

'What do you mean?' asked Elf Girl.

'I think we've found her.'

Raven Boy knelt down and picked up the thing he'd seen lying on the cave floor.

It was a small glass bottle, and inside it, was a tiny figure, a young woman in fact.

She was staring at them through the glass as Raven Boy held the bottle up to their faces, and she looked cross, very cross indeed.

'Fancy that,' said Elf Girl. 'Jean's a genie.'

Nine

aven Boy can't believe how
ot the desert is. He likes a
ce cool forest to hang about
in where sand isn't always
getting in your ears.

Jean the genie might have been tiny,
but she looked very cross, and even though she
was stuck inside a glass bottle with a cork in the
top, Raven Boy and Elf Girl were scared of her
already.

She was waving her arms about inside
the bottle and although they couldn't hear what
she was saying, or read her lips, they could tell

she was hopping mad.

'Not surprising,' said Elf Girl. 'Shut up inside a bottle.'

'I wonder why the Sandpeople didn't mention it,' said Raven Boy.

'What?' asked Elf Girl. 'That she's in a bottle? I expect it slipped their minds.'

'Rather an important fact to forget, wouldn't you say?' said Raven Boy.

'There's only one thing for it, we have to let her out.'

'Are you sure that's a good idea?' asked Raven Boy.

'I don't know if it's a good idea but it's our only choice. We need to speak to Jean and unless she and you both know sign language then we need to let her out.'

Inside the bottle, Jean was waving her arms around all the more fiercely.

'Do you think she can hear what we're saying? Maybe we can write notes and hold them up to the glass?'

'Oh for goodness' sake,' cried Elf Girl, and with that, she pulled the cork out of the bottle.

There was a rather cool flash of light and a puff of purple and green smoke, and next second Jean stood before them, full-sized.

Full-sized Jean however turned out not to be that big. She just about reached Elf Girl's shoulder. She was plump, and had her hair tied up in a long pigtail. What she lacked in height, she made up for in grumpiness.

'About time!' she moaned. 'Have you any idea how long I've been stuck in that bottle?'

'It's not our fault!' said Elf Girl.

Raven Boy had a vision of Elf Girl and Jean getting into a fight, and decided to calm things down.

'You're out now,' he said. 'So all's well.'

'All's well?' roared Jean. 'All's well! Who do you think you are?! Telling me my business. All is far from well! I've been stuck in that bottle for a decade, give or take a year, and you tell me everything's okay! Let me assure you . . .'

'We didn't have to let you out, you

know,' interrupted Elf Girl. 'And it wasn't our fault you were in there in the first place. You ought to be grateful!'

Jean stopped and looked rather sour as she muttered something so quietly that they couldn't hear her.

'Pardon?' asked Elf Girl.

'I said, yes, you're right. Unfortunately, since you let me out of my bottle, you have the right to three wishes, which I shall grant you.'

'Three wishes?' cried Elf Girl. 'That's brilliant! Are you sure?'

'Of course I'm sure!' snapped Jean. 'I am a genie, after all. It's what I do. Only be careful with your wishes, because most people make an utter foul-up of it.'

Elf Girl looked at Raven Boy.

'Wow!' she said.

'How does it work?' asked Raven Boy.

'Just take the bottle and make your wishes,' said Jean.

'Fantastic!' cried Raven Boy. 'Here, give me the bottle. I know what to do. I've often thought about this.'

'You have?' asked Elf Girl.

Raven Boy snatched the bottle from Elf Girl.

'Oh yes,' he said. 'I have.'

'Wait, Raven Boy . . .' began Elf Girl, but it was too late.

Raven Boy made his first wish.

'I wish for a thousand wishes!' he declared.

Jean groaned.

'See! What a great wish!' said Raven Boy. Then he added, 'Has it worked?'

Jean tapped the bottle with her fingernail.

'Should have read the small print,' she said. 'One wish wasted!'

'The what?' asked Raven Boy, with a bad feeling in his stomach.

'The small print,' said Jean, with a rather unpleasant smile on her face. 'On the bottom of the bottle.'

'Oh, Raven Boy!' groaned Elf Girl, snatching the bottle from Raven Boy. 'I wish you weren't always so stupid!'

Then she clapped her hand over her mouth.

'Elf Girl!' shouted Raven Boy.

'Too late!' laughed Jean. 'That's two wishes gone. See what I mean. Everyone makes a mess of it. Every time!'

Raven Boy and Elf Girl glared at Jean, and then at each other.

'Don't say another word,' said Raven Boy, and Elf Girl nodded. 'Until we've read the small print.'

'Good idea,' said Elf Girl, then clapped

her hand over her mouth again.

Together, they read the small print in silence.

1. Wishes may not refer to the wishing process itself. E.g. you cannot wish for more wishes.

'Look!' said Elf Girl, 'It mentions me! E.g. That's Elf Girl.'

'Don't be silly,' said Raven Boy. 'It means "for example".'

'Then why doesn't it say "F.e."?' asked Elf Girl.

'It's Latin, isn't it,' said Raven Boy. 'Exempli gratia.'

Elf Girl stared at Raven Boy.

'Since when do you know Latin?' she asked.

'Shh,' said Raven Boy. 'Let's read the rest of the small print first.'

2. Wishes may not refer to the genie in the bottle.

3. Wishes are irrevocable.

'What does that mean?' asked Elf Girl.

'They cannot be undone,' explained Raven Boy.

Elf Girl stared at Raven Boy.

'You're very smart all of a sudden . . .'

'Shh!' hushed Raven Boy. 'Let's finish reading.'

'And get on with it,' muttered Jean. 'I've got places to go, people to see. Been stuck in a bottle for ten years, and I think I left a casserole cooking at home.'

They ignored her and finished reading the small print, which was very small indeed and printed on a titchy label on the bottom of the bottle.

4. The manufacturers of this bottle may not be held accountable for any situation, deadly or otherwise, arising from the use of the wishes. We are not responsible for the outcome of your wishes, so watch it! Got it?

'Well,' said Raven Boy. 'That seems a little harsh.'

'Listen, Raven Boy, we have to think very carefully about this. We only have one wish left. We'd better make it a good one. Although . . .'

'What?' asked Raven Boy, but Elf Girl never answered, because just then a terrible

roar, a huge rumbling growl that filled the cave,
deafened them.

Their heads ringing, Elf Girl and Raven
Boy spun round to see a giant cave lion pounding
towards them, its jaws open, showing them a
lovely set of long sharp fangs.

'EEEEP!' wailed Raven Boy, as the lion
leapt towards them.

TEN

en Boy has noticed there
five different colours for
Girl's ears when she gets
ngry, from slightly pink
through to bright red.
He's only seen her
that mad once and
doesn't want to again.

The lion was enormous, and about as
angry and hungry as any lion ever was. It was
already in mid-leap as Raven Boy wailed, falling
backwards in fright, and Elf Girl did the only
thing she could.

She clutched the bottle tightly and shouted.
'I wish that lion was gone!'

And it was. Vanished into thin air. Just like that.

Jean sighed.

'There you go, three wishes all done. Pleasure doing business with you.'

Raven Boy was lying on the floor still, but jumped to his feet.

'Now just a minute,' he said.

'Don't you just a minute me,' said Jean. 'You had your three wishes and you blew it. That's all I have to do, give you three wishes for letting me out of the bottle and then I'm free.'

'All right,' cried Raven Boy, 'but before you go, please just tell us one thing.'

'Why should I?' said Jean.

She began waving her hands in the air, and Raven Boy watched in amazement as the cave began to disappear around them.

Suddenly they were standing in the hot desert once more, and Jean fluttered into the air like a fairy, ready to fly away.

'Please!' cried Elf Girl. 'Please, we have to ask you something!'

'We need to know how to find the

Tears of the Moon,' added Raven Boy, 'and the Singing Sword!'

'Oh yes?' asked Jean. 'Why should I tell you?'

'Because we have to know!'

'Because we have to fight the Goblin King, and we need them!'

'Because we were really rubbish at the three wishes,' wailed Elf Girl, 'and it's just not fair!'

Jean stared at them.

'Oh, very well, you were very bad at the three wishes, though I must say, that was quick thinking with the cave lion. Most people get eaten.'

'Thank you,' said Elf Girl, 'now please tell us. Please?'

'The Tears of the Moon and the Singing Sword?' she asked. 'It's very easy. Wait till the moon comes up, and then walk towards it. Keep walking towards it as it moves through the night, and when the sun comes up again, sit and wait until the following night. Eventually, you'll come to an oasis in the desert.'

'What's an oasis?' asked Elf Girl.

Raven Boy explained.

'It's a pool of water and usually a clutch of trees, found rarely in the desert but vital to those who travel through it.'

Elf Girl stared at him again.

'Quite right,' said Jean. 'Anyway, the Tears of the Moon is the water in the oasis. It's magical stuff. And the Singing Sword is stuck at the top of a tree that grows from the pool. That's all!'

She lifted higher into the air and waved.

'Listen, thanks for setting me free,' she said, and seemed to be in a much better mood now she wasn't cooped up in the bottle or for that matter, the cave.

'You're welcome,' said Raven Boy.

'There's just one more thing,' said Jean, laughing. 'Look out! The oasis isn't as lovely as it might seem! Beware!'

And with that, she flew away, with Raven Boy and Elf Girl calling after her.

'Why?'

'What is it? What's so dangerous?'

But Jean the genie had gone, leaving them with the small glass bottle and their pink parasols, which lay on the desert floor a little way away.

'What a weird episode that was!' said Raven Boy. 'What a shame we wasted our three wishes! We could have just wished for the Goblin King to be dead, and then wished to go home, and still have one wish left over.'

He hung his head, looking sad.

'I'm sorry I'm so stupid, Elf Girl,' he said. 'It was my fault.'

'No,' said Elf Girl, 'it was as much my fault.'

'You saved us from that lion,' said Raven Boy. 'It's just a shame we wasted the first two.'

'I'm not so sure that we did,' said Elf Girl. 'Waste them, I mean. Well, the first one, yes, but the second one . . .'

'About me not always being so stupid?' asked Raven Boy.

'Yes,' said Elf Girl. 'Haven't you noticed? Since I made that wish, you've spoken Latin and explained words I've never even heard of. Maybe it wasn't all wasted.'

'You mean, maybe it came true?'

'She didn't say it hadn't worked, did she?'

'So I'm going to be smarter than I was

before?' cried Raven Boy, getting excited.

'Yes,' said Elf Girl. 'Only . . .'

'Only what . . . ?'

'Only not always. That's what I said. Not always so stupid. So sometimes you're going to be smart, and others you're going to be normal.'

'Normal?' asked Raven Boy.

'Normal for you,' said Elf Girl, laughing. 'Which is to say, a total bird brain.'

'That's not funny,' said Raven Boy, but secretly he didn't care. Even the thought of being super-smart some of the time had cheered him up no end.

ELEVEN

aven Boy wasn't scared of
thing much before his tree
as pulled down by one of
the Goblin King's ogres.
Now he's discovered
the world is full of
scary things.

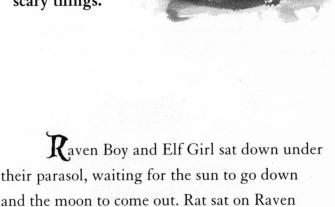

Raven Boy and Elf Girl sat down under
their parasol, waiting for the sun to go down
and the moon to come out. Rat sat on Raven
Boy's head, panting, because it was still so hot.

To pass the time, Elf Girl had decided to
see if Raven Boy really had become less stupid.

'What's five fives?' she asked.

'What?' blinked Raven Boy.

'What's five fives?'

'I don't understand the question.'

Elf Girl sighed.

'What's five times five?'

'Five times five?'

'So you're a parrot now, bird boy?'

'What?' asked Raven Boy, getting more and more confused.

'Listen,' said Elf Girl. 'Say you had picked up five nuts in the woods one day.'

'What kind of nuts?' asked Raven Boy.

Elf Girl's ear began to glow. Maybe it was the heat, or maybe she was getting worked up.

'It doesn't matter what kind of nuts!' she cried. 'Say you had five nuts and I said I'd swap them with you for five times as many berries. How many berries would you have?'

'What kind of berries?' asked Raven Boy, feeling hungry all of a sudden.

Elf Girl screamed.

'It doesn't matter what kind of berries!'

She glared at Raven Boy and then fell backwards in the sand, letting the parasol hide her face.

'I think you're just as stupid as you always were,' she muttered, grumpily.

'That's charming,' said Raven Boy. 'Anyway I think you're being unfair. I only wanted to know what kind of nuts and berries you were talking about. That kind of stuff is important in the forest. Some berries can make your stomach hurt for days, and you mustn't eat some kinds of nuts without roasting them first or your hair falls out.'

Elf Girl sat up again.

'Maybe you are a bit smarter than before,' she said.

'Of course I am,' said Raven Boy. 'Which is not to say that I was stupid before, either. Is it?'

He looked very hard at Elf Girl until she nodded.

'I'm sorry,' she said. 'You're right. You're not stupid. You're just . . .'

'Elf Girl!' interrupted Raven Boy. 'Don't spoil it now. You were managing to be nice for a minute. Let's keep it that way.'

Elf Girl sighed.

'You're right again,' she said. 'I'm sorry. It's just that I am very fed up of sitting around in hot sand all day.'

Raven Boy didn't answer, but suddenly stood up.

'We don't have to sit around any longer,' he said. 'Look!'

He pointed to the sky, where the sun was starting to set, and to where, over in the other side of the sky, the moon had risen and was already visible.

'Come on!' said Raven Boy. 'We may as well get going.'

They started to walk towards the moon.

'Listen,' said Elf Girl after a few minutes. 'The moon moves,

doesn't it? Through the night?'

'Yes,' said Raven Boy. 'It does.'

'So we're not going to walk in a straight line if we follow it, are we?'

'I think that's the point,' said Raven Boy. 'We follow the moon and eventually it will lead us to the right place.'

'But we'll walk in a circle,' said Elf Girl.

'No,' said Raven Boy. 'Actually we'll walk in a curve, the exact shape of which will depend upon our speed over the course of the night.'

'A which to the what?' asked Elf Girl, scratching her head. Then she added, 'Never mind! You see, you are smarter than you were before.'

Raven Boy stopped walking.

'Yes, maybe I am,' he said.

'Did you actually understand anything you just said?' asked Elf Girl.

'Yes,' said Raven Boy. 'Maybe . . . Possibly . . . No.'

He blinked.

'But it sounded right, didn't it? At least, it felt right, when I said it.'

Elf Girl pointed at the moon.

'That way?'

'That way,' agreed Raven Boy, and they set off again.

The sun set and darkness started to creep across the desert floor once more. The moon climbed slowly into the sky and Raven Boy and Elf Girl followed it carefully, always heading towards it, as it moved across the stars.

It was amazing how many stars there were in the desert, and there was more than enough light to see by as they went on their way.

It was much cooler than walking in the daytime too, and finally they began to feel they might be getting somewhere on their adventure. But if they were happier walking at night, they were also a little more scared, because out in the desert, in the darkness beyond the range of their sight, they could hear all sorts of creatures moving.

They had no idea what was out there, but some things sounded big, and some small. There were scuttling noises and slithering noises, there were howls and squeaks, and once there was a loud roar, which made them shiver in their boots.

Fortunately, the roar sounded a long way off, but it didn't make Raven Boy and Elf Girl feel like slowing down, so they headed on, into the night, until finally the moon set and there was still no sign of the oasis.

'I guess that's all for tonight,' said Elf Girl.

Raven Boy nodded.

'We'll try again tomorrow night,' he said.

They settled down to wait for dawn and

for the next night to come around, and neither of them dared say what they were thinking, which was that they were tired, hungry and thirsty, and they still had no idea how much further there was to go.

TWELVE

When Elf Girl was small she used to have a pet rabbit called Snuff. He was stupid. For some reason, Raven Boy reminds her of him.

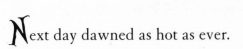

Next day dawned as hot as ever.

Raven Boy, Elf Girl and Rat lay under their parasols feeling like fish under a grill.

'I wonder if it ever rains here,' moaned Raven Boy.

'Shh,' said Elf Girl. 'Be quiet. I need all my energy just to breathe.'

'Goblin King,' said Raven Boy.

'What?' asked Elf Girl, looking scared and sitting up.

'Sorry,' said Raven Boy. 'You can lie down again. I meant it's all his fault. This desert. The whole world will end up like this if no one stops him.'

'I know,' said Elf Girl. 'But it's too hot to stop him right now.'

So they waited till the sun went down once again, and then set off towards the moon as they had before.

But the moon set and the sun came up again and there was still no sign of the oasis, nor of anything else for that matter.

They lay down and shut their eyes.

'Raven Boy,' whispered Elf Girl.

'What?'

'I think we're going to die here.'

Raven Boy nodded feebly.

'Good idea.'

Rat squeaked, but it was a weak little noise and no one heard him.

He tried again a bit louder, and still they didn't hear him.

So then he bit Raven Boy's nose.

'Ow!' wailed Raven Boy. 'What did you

do . . . ?'

He didn't finish his sentence, because he saw at once why Rat had done it.

There were scorpions. Thousands of them. Maybe tens of thousands, heading towards them over the sand.

'EEEP!' wailed Raven Boy, and he tugged Elf Girl to her feet.

'Run!'

The scorpions were catching up, and though they were small, they moved very fast. Then Elf Girl wailed and pointed to the left.

'Look!'

Raven Boy screamed and pointed to the right.

'EEEP!'

The scorpions were on either side of them, as well as behind them, giving them only one place to run, which was straight ahead.

From out of the heat haze in front of them, they saw a shimmering palace appear in the sand, blocking the way that they were running.

'Oh no!' gasped Elf Girl.

The palace was huge and they couldn't see a way in, or a way around it, as the scorpions closed in on all sides.

'Ignore it!' cried Raven Boy. 'It's just another one of those mirages!'

'Yes! You're right,' called Elf Girl.

'Thank goodness you're smart now!'

So they ran straight at the palace, expecting it to disappear.

It didn't, and they banged their heads on its hard stone walls, and bounced backwards onto their bottoms.

'Ow!' shouted Elf Girl. 'Raven Boy, you are just as stupid as ever.'

'Never mind that! We're trapped!'

Raven Boy stood with his back to the palace wall, and Elf Girl joined him. The scorpions had slowed down now they had trapped their prey. They inched slowly forward, waving their pincers and pointing their stinging tails towards Elf Girl and Raven Boy, who shivered as if they were made of jelly, despite the heat.

'Oh Raven Boy,' sniffed Elf Girl. 'I don't like things that hurt. Tell me it won't hurt.'

Raven Boy didn't say anything at all, because suddenly a hidden door opened in the wall behind them, and a pair of strong hands grabbed them by the scruffs of their necks, and pulled them inside.

There was the sound of the door slamming shut behind them, followed by a loud scuttling noise outside.

It was dark inside, and now that Raven Boy and Elf Girl were out of the bright sunlight it took a while for their eyes to adjust. When they did, they found themselves looking up at a tall strong man dressed very strangely.

He was wearing curly-toed shoes, which Elf Girl thought must have been because he had let his best pointy boots get wet. He had baggy silk trousers like pyjamas, and a red waistcoat – like a monkey would wear, thought Raven Boy.

On his bald head he wore a funny red hat with a black tassel dangling off the top.

He pointed at Raven Boy and Elf Girl and then pointed down the corridor in which they were standing.

'I think he wants us to go that way,' whispered Elf Girl to Raven Boy, gripping her bow tightly.

The man pointed at them again and then at the corridor. He was very tall, and he had muscles in places where Raven Boy didn't even have places. He didn't smile.

'Let's do what he says.'

'He didn't say anything,' whispered Elf Girl.

'Shh,' said Raven Boy. 'Just get going.'

So they set off into the palace, which they soon saw was a fabulous place, with posh floors made of polished stone, and fine columns that were decorated with carvings. The ceilings were high, and as they wandered through room after room, they saw that they were all painted with fantastic scenes of weird creatures, things that Elf Girl wasn't even sure existed, apart from maybe in story books.

The big silent man still hadn't
said anything, but he grabbed them
by the scruffs of their necks and
made them stop outside a door so
enormous it must have taken half
a tree to make it. Half a big tree,
thought Raven Boy sadly.

The silent man banged
on the door, making a noise like
thunder in the mountains, and then he
pushed the door open.

Beyond was a room so
ornate, so richly decorated and
simply so huge that Elf Girl and
Raven Boy's mouths fell open. Even
Rat twisted something in his neck trying to see
how high the ceiling was.

At the very, very far end of the room,
which was very, very far away, was a throne,
and on the throne sat a king, surrounded by
more people all dressed like the big silent man,
but just not quite as big as him.

The door slammed behind them.

'EEEP!' cheeped Raven Boy.

THIRTEEN

When he's sleeping in the forest, Raven Boy sometimes makes a nice soft bed out of fresh branches of fir and moss. Perfect for napping.

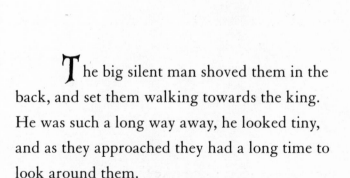

The big silent man shoved them in the back, and set them walking towards the king. He was such a long way away, he looked tiny, and as they approached they had a long time to look around them.

The walls were covered in wild paintings, shimmering with gold, and there were cool pools of water with fountains playing on all sides.

The room was lined with servants, and there, still a long way ahead of them, was the king.

At least they assumed he was a king.

He was sitting on a throne of gold, and he had a pointy ring of gold on his head, and that meant he was a king as far as Elf Girl and Raven Boy were concerned.

He was quite old, but as they got closer they could see he still looked tall and strong. His beard was long and narrow and reached his knees, he wore fine silken robes and that nifty crown.

Next to him, on a slightly smaller throne made of silver, was someone who was probably his queen. She wore equally fine clothes, and had a slightly smaller silvery crown on her head. She was also tall, and very beautiful, so beautiful that Raven Boy found it hard to stop staring at her.

Elf Girl nudged him in the ribs.

'Hey,' she hissed. 'Bird boy. Leave this to me.'

'Hmm?' said Raven Boy, tearing his eyes away from the queen.

Elf Girl stepped forward in front of the king and queen, whose thrones were high above them on a platform of marble so smooth and shiny you could see your face in it.

'Hello,' she said. 'I'm Elf Girl and this is Raven Boy and we have a small rodent with us somewhere, most likely in Raven Boy's pocket. Listen, we're very grateful to you for saving us.

You've no idea how miserable it's been. We've been wandering for days without food or water and then there were those terrible scorpions outside your castle. And really, it would be lovely if we could have something to eat now. Please. Thank you.'

Elf Girl stopped.

She had the feeling it wasn't going well. The king and queen stared down at them with faces that could have been made of stone.

Raven Boy pulled Elf Girl back.

'Let me try,' he said, nervously. He grinned at the queen. She didn't grin back.

'Please, your kingliness and queensomeness . . .'

He didn't get any further than that.

'Stop!' roared the king in a surprisingly loud voice. He held his hand in the air, and there was total silence in the hall. Even the fountains seemed to decide it might be better to dry up for a bit.

Raven Boy took a step back to huddle next to Elf Girl, and they both began to walk backwards, until they knocked into something.

Looking up, they saw the face of the big silent man, looking down at them. Unlike the couple on the throne, he did grin, but somehow it wasn't very nice when he did.

The king snorted.

'You!' he said. 'Let me tell you something. I am not a king! I am the Sultan! The Sultan of Dread Desert. Not a king! How dare you insult me!'

Raven Boy coughed very quietly.

'I'm really sorry,' he said. 'I just thought you and your queen here . . .'

'Enough!' roared the Sultan. 'Queen? Queen! This is no queen. I am the Sultan and this is the Sultana!'

Raven Boy and Elf Girl burst out laughing.

'Sultana!' they both chortled. 'That's a good one. You set us up for that!'

They chuckled and chortled and muttered 'Sultana!' quite a lot.

Raven Boy pointed at the big silent man behind them.

'He's your raisin, I suppose?' he said, keeping a straight face for a split second, and then he and Elf Girl collapsed in another fit of the giggles.

'Looks more like a dried prune to me!' spluttered Elf Girl.

They kept on laughing and giggling, and then Raven Boy noticed that Elf Girl had gone quiet. In fact, she was nudging him in the ribs, and then nodding at the Sultan and Sultana.

The Sultan looked so cross you could almost see steam coming out of his ears.

'So,' he said, slowly, and very menacingly. 'You come into my desert, you insult me and you insult the Sultana. . .'

Raven Boy started to giggle again. He made a strange splurting noise as he tried to stop, and Elf Girl stamped on his toes for good measure.

'And now . . .' continued the Sultan, 'you

will pay the price! Hakim!'

The silent man stood to attention, waiting for instructions.

'Hakim! Take them to the cells underneath the palace! Make sure they are made very uncomfortable, while I decide whether to throw them into the crocodile pit or just cut their heads straight off! Go!'

'No!' wailed Raven Boy.

'You can't do that!' screamed Elf Girl.

'Wait!' cried Raven Boy. 'You can't do this. I'm sorry we were rude to you but you have to help us! We're on a special mission, you see. We're trying to save the world from the Goblin King!'

Suddenly, the Sultan stood up and waved a hand at Hakim, to tell him to stop hauling them out of the hall.

'You are, are you?' said the Sultan. 'You're going to save the world from the Goblin King?'

'Yes!' said Elf Girl. 'Yes, so you have to set us free, you have to help us!'

'Now why would I want to do that?'

asked the Sultan. 'The Goblin King is my master!'

Raven Boy and Elf Girl looked at each other, horrified.

'No!'

'Oh, yes!' said the Sultan. 'I serve the Goblin King, and I think he'd be very interested to know about you two. Hakim, take them away!'

Hakim dragged Raven Boy and Elf Girl away and threw them into a dank, dark cell, from which there was no possible way of escape.

FOURTEEN

rolls might seem vicious
nd stupid but that's not
tually what they are like.
ey're actually vicious and
stupid and ugly.

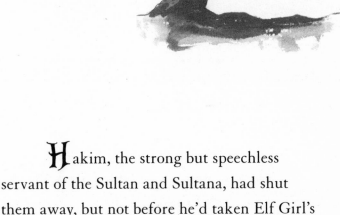

Hakim, the strong but speechless
servant of the Sultan and Sultana, had shut
them away, but not before he'd taken Elf Girl's
bow away, all without saying a word.

They were locked in a tiny cell, with one
door, through which they'd come, and no windows.
The door had a small window in it, but it was
covered by a grille.

Once Hakin had stomped off down the passageway, Raven Boy tried the handle of the door.

It didn't budge.

'Just thought I'd check,' he said. 'Oh, Elf Girl, we've really done it this time.'

'I know,' said Elf Girl. 'We only laughed in the face of the Goblin King's best friend.'

They both felt terrified at the thought.

'And now he's going to tell the Goblin King we've been trying to find him. That's not good.'

'I know that too,' said Elf Girl.

They sat down sadly and didn't say anything for a long time.

Finally, Raven Boy spoke.

'Well,' he said.

'Yes?' said Elf Girl. 'Come up with a plan, have you?'

'Er, no,' said Raven Boy. 'I was just going to say at least it's cool down here.'

'Oh, Raven Boy!' cried Elf Girl. 'Can't you do better than that? Can't you have one of your new super-smart spells and think of a way out?'

Raven Boy shook his head.

'Sorry,' he said. 'But I'm not feeling very clever just now. I'm feeling hungry and scared, and that's not a great combination for feeling smart.'

Rat popped his head out of Raven Boy's pocket.

He squeaked and Raven Boy nodded.

'Yes, that's not bad,' he said. He turned to Elf Girl. 'Rat says he could get out through the grille on the door, and go and see what's what.'

Elf Girl nodded.

'He's not going to be able to get us out of here though, is he?'

Rat gave a cross little squeak.

'No offence, Rat,' said Elf Girl. 'I just think we're stuck here, that's all. At least until they cut our heads off.'

'Or throw us in the crocodile pit,' added Raven Boy. He stroked Rat between his ears.

'Listen, Rat,' he said. 'If there's the slightest chance you can get out of here and save yourself, you must, do you understand?'

Now Rat squeaked very loudly indeed, and Raven Boy's eyes filled with tears.

'What is it?' asked Elf Girl, very gently.

'He says he's not going anywhere without us,' sniffed Raven Boy and then Elf Girl gave Rat a big kiss on the top of his head.

'Go and see what's happening, Rat,' she said. 'And see if you can find something to eat too.'

Raven Boy held Rat up to the bars of the

window and he shot through and scampered
off down the corridor straight away, sniffing
this way and that, because Rats are very good at
finding food with their noses.

'Maybe they won't cut our heads off yet,'
said Raven Boy.

'Why not?' asked Elf Girl.

'Because the Sultan wants to tell the Goblin
King about us. Maybe he wants to find out what
to do with us. That could take some time.'

'Maybe,' said Elf Girl. 'It depends.'

'On what?'

'On how they speak to each other,' she
said. 'Maybe they have crystal balls they use to
communicate, like Jeremy the wizard did in
Monster Mountains.'

Raven Boy nodded gloomily.

'You're right,' he said. 'But you never
know. Maybe they have to write to each other,
and send the messages by birds.'

'Perhaps. Or even better, by camel.'

'A camel with a wonky leg,' said Raven
Boy, grinning, and despite their dismal situation,
they both smiled.

They waited a long time for Rat to get back, and when he did, he was dragging a large piece of cheese in his teeth, which with great difficulty he managed to pull up the outside of the cell door, and pop through the window.

He tumbled in after it, as Elf Girl and Raven Boy cheered.

'Yay!'

'Well done, Rat!' they cried, and then they shared the cheese between them.

Rat squeaked, and told Raven Boy he'd managed to get to the kitchens and have a snack himself before stealing the cheese.

'Well done, Rat!' Raven Boy said again, and Rat squeaked again, and Raven Boy stopped chewing and went white.

'What is it?' said Elf Girl desperately. 'What did he say?'

Raven Boy swallowed before he spoke. '**Meep!**' he said.

Elf Girl wailed.

'Raven Boy! What is it?'

'Rat said he came back through the big hall where we were before. He said he heard the Sultan speaking to the Sultana. He said that the Goblin King has told him not to kill us.'

'But that's good news,' said Elf Girl. 'Isn't it?'

'It would be, if it wasn't for what the Sultan said next. He said the Goblin King is going to come here.'

'Come here! Why?' wailed Elf Girl.

'So he can kill us himself.'

And with that Elf Girl fainted and Raven Boy could think of nothing better to do than to join her.

FIFTEEN

The desert is the most boring place Elf Girl has ever been. In fact, the only interesting thing about it is how full of dangerous things it is, and that's not something to be happy about.

When they came round, it was to the sound of Rat sniffing, licking their faces and generally doing cute things that might wake them up.

Raven Boy opened his eyes and smiled when he saw Rat. Then he remembered that the Goblin King was coming to kill them, and fainted again.

Rat gave a tiny little snort that sounded like a sigh, and started licking Raven Boy's nose again.

Some time later, Elf Girl and Raven Boy stood at the door to their cell, staring out of the window, terrified at what they might see.

What they hoped to see was Rat returning with a key. They'd sent their small friend off once more, desperately hoping that he might be able to find some way of letting them out.

What they didn't want to see was Hakim, or the Sultan, or worst of all, the terrible Goblin King, coming down the passage, looking as though he wanted to chop heads and break bones.

Suddenly they saw Rat scuttling towards the door once more.

They were pleased to see him, but disappointed that he was empty-mouthed. No key, not even a piece of cheese this time.

And their happiness at seeing him at all turned into fright when they heard footsteps, and there was the Sultana walking quickly towards them.

'EEEP!' cried Raven Boy. 'They've come

to cut off our heads!'

'And throw us to the crocodiles!'

The Sultana did something very strange. She picked a key from somewhere in her silken robes, unlocked the door, and pushed it open.

Raven Boy and Elf Girl stood staring at her.

'Be quick about it!' she whispered.

'About what?' asked Raven Boy.

'You really are as stupid as you look,' said the Sultana. She sighed. 'Be quick about escaping, that's what. You don't have much time. The Goblin King is on his way.'

Raven Boy and Elf Girl stared at each other.

'You're helping us?' asked Elf Girl. 'But you're . . . you're . . .'

'Yes?' asked the Sultana.

'You're the Sultana!' said Elf Girl, eventually.

'And don't I know it!' the Sultana said, rather huffily. 'I've had it with him.'

'Who?' asked Raven Boy.

'The Sultan, that's who. Honestly! What kind of name is that? Oh, it was different when we met, of course. In those days he was young and handsome and said he owned a desert, which I thought was tremendously romantic.'

Elf Girl and Raven Boy stared at the Sultana, but she hadn't finished yet.

'Let me tell you, sand is not romantic. There's absolutely nothing to do here except order people about all day and I'm bored! I can't stand it. He's always shouting at people and chopping their heads off. So I'm going to help you escape, but please be quick about it before any one sees us!'

'Er, right,' said Raven Boy, who was having trouble not staring at the Sultana again, because she was so beautiful.

'My,' said the Sultana, 'you are a little cutie-pie, aren't you?'

She winked at Raven Boy, who nearly fainted, until Elf Girl stepped on his toes, and made a loud humphing noise.

Even in the dark Raven Boy could see Elf Girl's ears were turning pink, so he grabbed her by the hand and dragged her from the cell.

'Which way shall we go?' he asked the Sultana.

'Follow me,' she whispered. 'I have a plan.'

They followed the Sultana along the
dimly lit corridor, but something was bothering
Raven Boy.

'Er, Mrs Sultana,' he whispered.

'Yes, what is it?' the Sultana whispered
back, pausing at a corner to check the coast was
clear.

'We're very sorry we laughed at your
name. We didn't mean to be rude.'

'Oh that!' said the Sultana. 'Don't worry,

I couldn't agree with you more. It's one more thing I hate about him. He didn't tell me I had to be called the Sultana when I married him. Oh no. You had every right to laugh! I thought I was going to snigger myself watching you two!'

Here, she smiled at Raven Boy, who thought he might faint with excitement, but Elf Girl gently reminded him to get a move on by kicking his backside with her pointy boots.

'Mrs Sultana,' she said, politely. 'You wouldn't know where my bow has gone, would you? It's very important to me and we're lost without it.'

'Why yes, as it happens, I do. It's been locked away in the armoury, which is next door to where I'm taking you.'

'So can we get it back? Do you have a key for the armoury?'

'Of course I do. I am the Sultana after all.'

She smiled at Elf Girl, who felt better herself under the Sultana's lovely smile.

'But won't you get in a lot of trouble when the Sultan finds out we're missing?'

'Oh don't you worry about that,' said the Sultana, 'I can wrap him round my little finger.'

Raven Boy stared at her, looking worried.

'That just means he does whatever I want him to,' said the Sultana, laughing.

'But what about the Goblin King?' asked

Elf Girl.

The Sultana looked a little doubtful.

'I've never met him but he can't be that bad, can he?'

Elf Girl and Raven Boy looked at each other, and decided to say nothing. The last thing they wanted was to scare the Sultana into locking them both up again.

'Now!' she said. 'Here we are! The armoury is over there, and here . . .' she swung open another door, 'is the flying carpet room.'

'Flying . . .?' said Raven Boy.

'. . . carpet?' said Elf Girl.

The Sultana smiled, and nodded.

'Oh,' said Raven Boy. 'Yes. Yes, yes, yes!'

Sixteen

Sometimes, when it rains in the forest, Raven Boy takes shelter in a cave or a badger's sett, but mostly he just takes the chance to have a shower and get clean.

'Which one would you like?' asked the Sultana.

Raven Boy stood staring at the flying carpet room. Elf Girl was stroking her bow as if it was a long-lost kitten, and the Sultana was locking the armoury door once more.

The room was like a carpet shop, with rugs of all sizes and patterns spread out on the floor, but absolutely nothing seemed magical about any of them.

Rat squeaked doubtfully.

'Hmm, what?' asked Elf Girl.

'Oh,' said Raven Boy, 'He said, "Why are we getting excited about a room full of rugs?"'

'He has a point, actually,' said Elf Girl.

'But they fly!' said Raven Boy.

'Do they?' asked Elf Girl. 'They don't look very floaty . . .'

The Sultana looked irritated.

'Do you think you could get on with it? Anyone might come at any minute and then I'll be in trouble and you'll be dead.'

Raven Boy blinked in his bird-like way.

'Are you sure they fly?' he asked, starting to doubt it himself. It was just so easy to want to believe everything the Sultana said, but the more he thought about it, the more he doubted it.

'Just pick one, will you?' snapped the Sultana. 'Heavens! Why is it so hard to help you people escape?'

'Sorry,' muttered Raven Boy, and pointed at the nearest carpet. 'That one.'

'Take your time about it,' sighed the Sultana.

'Why?' asked Elf Girl. 'They're all the same.'

'My dear girl,' said the Sultana. 'Do you know anything about flying carpets? Obviously not. If you did, you would not have said such an ignorant thing. Each carpet has a mind of its own. Its own personality. Its own special little ways. Now that one, for example . . .'

She stopped, and her face suddenly froze

in fear.

'There's someone coming! Quick! Get on the carpet and get out of here.'

Raven Boy and Elf Girl leapt onto the carpet, which at once hovered a foot off the floor.

'Whoah!' cried Raven Boy. 'They do fly!'

'Do they?' asked Elf Girl, because although the rug was floating in the air, it had otherwise gone nowhere.

'Quick! Tell it where you want to go,' cried the Sultana. She pointed at the ceiling of the room, which was open to the sky. 'Off you go!'

'Wait!' said Raven Boy. 'What about the other carpets? They can follow us on those!'

'Leave them to me,' the Sultana cried.

She slammed the door to the carpet room, locking herself inside. She took an oil lamp from the wall and started to set light to the other carpets.

Raven Boy watched the Sultana helping them and felt very grateful. He pulled a sleek black feather from his hair and handed it to her, with a smile.

'Maybe you'll remember me,' he said. 'I mean us,' he added, hurriedly, seeing Elf Girl looking at him.

'Oh how sweet,' said the Sultana, and tucked the feather in the same place she kept her keys. 'Now will you please get a move on?'

Elf Girl was working hard on it.

'Er, carpet,' she said. 'Hello. Er, get us out of here.'

The carpet kept hovering but didn't budge forwards or higher up.

'No!' wailed the Sultana. 'Tell it where you want to go!'

'Oh,' said Raven Boy. 'Carpet, take us to the oasis known as the Tears of the Moon! Now!'

At once, a small woman appeared at the front end of the carpet, dressed just like the Sultan's other servants. She was no higher than Rat's tail was long, and she was sort of see-through, as if she wasn't really there.

'Repeat destination please,' she said in a bossy little voice.

'The Tears of the Moon! Now!' cried Raven Boy, and then the carpet shot up vertically through the open roof of the palace.

'Hold on tight!' shouted the Sultana, waving at them as they went, and setting light to the rest of the flying carpets.

Raven Boy and Elf Girl didn't need telling.

The carpet was hurtling at an unbelievable speed low across the sandy desert, and Raven Boy and Elf Girl were screaming for dear life, while Rat had dug all four sets of claws into the rug, terrified of being blown away.

Raven Boy dared to look backwards and spotted a column of smoke rising from the palace. He was hoping the Sultana would be all right when the little figure on the carpet began to speak again.

'Welcome aboard this magic carpet ride to the oasis known as the Tears of the Moon,' she said, not even seeming to notice the speed they were moving at. Her hair didn't blow about, her clothes didn't flap in the breeze.

'Flight time today is an estimated thirty-five minutes,' continued the carpet. 'My name is Shona and it's my pleasure to be looking after you today. In a little while I'll be serving a selection of hot and cold snacks and refreshments, but for the time being just sit back, relax, and enjoy the views.'

'What?' wailed Raven Boy.

'What views?' cried Elf Girl, and then she added, 'And who cares?'

They'd both managed to stop screaming, but it was all they could do to stay aboard the carpet, which if anything seemed to be getting faster all the time.

'Please!' shouted Raven Boy. 'Please! Shona! Please slow down.'

Shona appeared not to have heard him.

'In addition to our award-winning buffet service,' she said, 'it's my great pleasure to offer you the chance to get some great deals in our sky boutique. There are replica camels at half price, and a buy-one-get-one-free offer on boxes of dates . . .'

'Shona!' shouted Raven Boy again.

Shona stopped talking and glared at him.

'If you want to speak to me,' she said, 'you have to push the button in the panel above your head.'

'What button?' wailed Raven Boy. 'What panel?'

Shona glared at him even harder.

'Just pretend, okay,' she said, in a rather threatening voice.

So Raven Boy pretended to push a button in a panel which he pretended was above his head, and then Shona turned a big smile on.

'How may I help you, sir?' she said, showing him lots of neat white teeth.

'Please,' wailed Raven Boy, 'please slow down!'

'Very well, sir,' said Shona, and finally the carpet dropped its speed to something less life-threatening.

They now flew gently over the sand, and were able to sit up, and look around. Rat released his claws and re-joined Raven Boy, and Elf Girl even went as far as to stand up and look back the way they'd come.

In the far distance a thin column of smoke drifted into the blue desert sky.

'I think we're safe,' she said, clapping her hands. 'We got away!'

'Thanks to that lovely lady,' said Raven Boy. 'And Elf Girl, you know what?'

'What?'

'With this carpet, we'll be at the oasis in no time!'

'Due to reduced cruising speeds,' announced Shona, 'our corrected flight time today will be two and a half hours. This is due to matters out of our control.'

'Fine by me!' said Raven Boy, happily. 'Just time for a little nap before we get there, and then we can get on with saving the world!'

Elf Girl laughed, and then they lay down, putting Raven Boy's coat over their faces to shield themselves from the sun, while Shona droned on and on about special deals only available for a limited time on Magic Carpet Airways.

SEVENTEEN

Raven Boy thinks the desert is just about the stupidest place he's ever been, but it's only because he hasn't been to Terror Town yet.

'So what is it with you, anyway?' Raven Boy asked Shona, as they flew on. The sun was starting to set and the moon was already up.

Shona ignored him.

Raven Boy sighed and pretended to push a button.

'What is it with you?' he repeated.

'I'm sorry, sir, I'm not sure what you mean by that.'

Elf Girl rolled her eyes at Raven Boy.

'Don't bother,' she said. 'We're getting there, aren't we?'

Raven Boy pretended to push a button above his head.

'Shona, how much longer now?'

'We will start our descent in fifteen minutes.'

'Even I don't have a clue what she's talking about,' said Raven Boy, 'and I'm super-smart.'

'Sometimes,' said Elf Girl. 'You're super-smart sometimes. Don't forget that.'

'How could I, with you to remind me?' smiled Raven Boy, and he pinched Elf Girl somewhere he shouldn't have.

She jumped up and nearly fell over.

'Please remain seated until we have finished our descent,' snapped Shona.

'What?'

'She means sit down,' said Raven Boy, so Elf Girl did, and Shona gave her a very fake smile.

'So, what do we do?' asked Elf Girl.

'When we get to the oasis?'

Elf Girl rolled her eyes.

'Obviously,' she said, still not happy

about being pinched.

'Simple,' said Raven Boy. 'We grab some of the oasis water, nab the sword, and high-tail it out of there on the carpet.'

'Do we have to?' whispered Elf Girl. 'She's a sourpuss, isn't she?'

'I know,' whispered Raven Boy, who could see Shona staring at them. 'But it's much easier than walking through the desert.'

He smiled at Shona. She didn't smile back.

'Just one thing,' said Elf Girl.

'What's that?' asked Raven Boy.

'What are we going to put the water in?'

'Aha!' said Raven Boy, and rummaged in the pocket of his coat. He pulled out a familiar-looking empty glass bottle.

'Jean's bottle! Have you had that the whole time?' asked Elf Girl.

'Uh-huh,' nodded Raven Boy. 'It's just one of the things that us super-smart people do. Plan ahead.'

'And have you got anything else in there? A three-course dinner perhaps?'

Raven Boy gave Elf Girl a look and was about to say something really clever, when the carpet suddenly twitched and changed direction.

It began to head down ever so gently towards the desert. Elf Girl jumped up and down.

'Look!' she cried. 'Look! There it is! The Tears of the Moon!'

It was true. There, just a short way ahead, was an oasis of a few tall trees and a large pool of water, from which grew one even taller tree. Above the oasis, the moon hung high in the sky.

'Yay!' shouted Raven Boy and he began to jump up and down too.

Shona glared at them both.

'Passengers will please . . .'

'Oh shut up!' laughed Elf Girl, and as the carpet came to a graceful stop at the edge of the pool, she jumped onto the sand.

Raven Boy pushed a button in the air above his head.

'Shona. You are to stay here and wait for us. Understand?'

Shona said nothing.

'Understand?' asked Raven Boy again.

Shona nodded grumpily.

'I understand,' she muttered.

'Good!' shouted Raven Boy, and hopped onto the sand next to Elf Girl.

'Right then!' he said. 'Where's this sword then?'

'Er,' said Elf Girl. 'I think we have a problem here. Look! Isn't the sword supposed to be at the top of that tree?'

Raven Boy looked up at the top of the tree, but could see nothing.

'Maybe it's well hidden,' he said. 'Or very small?'

'Or maybe it's not there any more,' Elf Girl said.

'Well,' said Raven Boy. 'Let's get some of the water into the bottle, then we can shin up and have a proper look. Here!'

He handed the bottle to Elf Girl. She dipped it into the pool, just as Raven Boy began wading in towards the tree where the Singing Sword was supposed to be waiting.

Neither of them got very far, because as soon as they touched the water, a beast shot up out of it. It was like a snake, but as fat as six tree trunks and taller than them too.

It had two wild eyes that hunted them down, its mouth was full of long razor-sharp teeth, and it was very, very angry.

EIGHTEEN

lf Girl started wearing
nty boots when her mum
gave her a pair for her
rthday. Now she won't
ear anything else, even
hough they're getting
a bit tatty.

The water snake spotted Raven Boy
and lunged towards him.

'**EEEP!**' wailed Raven Boy, and rushed
back out of the water.

Elf Girl fell onto her bottom, and began
to scrabble backwards in the sand.

'Shoot it!' Raven Boy called to Elf Girl.
'Use your bow. Shoot it!'

Desperately, Elf Girl pulled her bow
from her belt and drew back the invisible string.

'Don't muck it up!' shouted Raven Boy.

'Shut up!' cried Elf Girl. 'That's not helpful!'

Raven Boy was too busy running for his
life. The beast snapped and sniped at him, and
he ducked and dived, trying to get away from it,
but all he ended up doing was running round in
circles in the sand.

Elf Girl fired her bow.

'Yay!' she cried, because once again, real
arrows flew from it, three at once.

Then she gasped in horror as the arrows hit the water snake and bounced off it.

'It didn't even tickle it!' she cried.

'Hurry!' shouted Raven Boy. 'Do something!'

Elf Girl fired again.

More arrows flew, but the result was the same.

The snake didn't even seem to notice it had been struck.

'Do something else!' cried Raven Boy, and he jumped back onto the magic carpet.

'Shona! Fly! Pick up Elf Girl and fly!'

The carpet shot off towards Elf Girl and scooped her up by zooming under her feet.

'Watch it!' she wailed, and the carpet began to fly around in tight circles following Raven Boy's instructions.

'Shoot it! Something other than arrows!' he called, and Elf Girl stood up and began to launch a volley of odd things at the snake.

First she fired a bunch of flowers, then an umbrella.

That was followed by a cloud of butterflies

and a snowstorm. None of them had any effect,
and all the while the neck and head of the snake
kept chasing them, writhing out of the water,
snapping at the carpet and at them.

'Try that again!' shouted Raven Boy.

'What?' shouted Elf Girl.

'The snow, but make it even colder!
Make it ice!'

So Elf Girl thought very hard, and the
arrow mark on her arm glowed very brightly as
she fired once more, and this time she didn't fire
at the beast, but at the pool of water itself.

Something icy and blue whizzed from

her bow, and seconds later, ice began to form on the oasis.

'Do it again!' cried Raven Boy, and she did.

She fired again and again, and each time the water began to freeze a little more, and then all at once, with a loud snapping sound, the whole pool was one large block of ice, with a giant frozen water snake sticking out of it.

'You did it!' cheered Raven Boy. 'You did it! You really know what you're doing!'

Elf Girl smiled and looked at her bow.

'Sort of!' she said. 'Sometimes, at least, I sort of do.'

'Come on!' shouted Raven Boy, and he got Shona to land again.

Being very careful to tell the rapid rug to wait, they sprinted over to the pool.

'There's just one problem now,' said Elf Girl, and tapped the bottle against the ice of the pool.

'Hmm,' said Raven Boy. 'Can you try and chip a piece out? Then we can melt it and drip it into the bottle.'

'I'll try,' Elf Girl said, soon finding a new use for her pointy-toed boots.

Rat collected all the little chips of ice, and popped them into the bottle, which was soon full.

Raven Boy meanwhile had shimmied over the ice and, being very good at climbing, was up the tree in the middle of the pool in no time at all.

He came back

162

down to find Elf Girl and Rat waiting for him.

'Well,' she said. 'No sword?'

Raven Boy shook his head.

'No sword,' he said. 'Just this.'

He held up a piece of paper.

Elf Girl read.

'"If you're looking for the Singing Sword, too bad. We borrowed it. Yours faithfully, Terrible Tim."'

Elf Girl shook her head.

'What! We've come all this way and someone's beaten us to it!'

'Terrible Tim?' wondered Raven Boy. 'Do you think that's T.T.? The owner of the grumpy camel?'

'Yes!' said Elf Girl. 'I think you're right. He was here before us.'

'Terrible Tim!' wailed Raven Boy. 'I don't think he sounds very nice, do you?'

Elf Girl shook her head.

'At least we have the Tears of the Moon,' she said, looking into the bottle. Inside it, the hot sun was already turning the chips of ice back into oasis water.

'We'd better get out of here before someone else thaws out too,' Raven Boy said.

'Agreed,' said Elf Girl. 'But what do we do then?'

Raven Boy pointed at the paper.

'We find Terrible Tim and we get the sword back.'

'Of course we do,' said Elf Girl, a little huffily. 'Only how do we find him?'

'Easy,' said Raven Boy. 'When you're super-smart. If you look closely you'll see that the paper has some other writing on it.'

Elf Girl looked again at the paper and saw that it had been taken from a hotel, in fact a hotel with a rather worrying sounding name.

'The Horror Hotel?' she read. 'The Horror Hotel of Terror Town? Oh, Raven Boy, I don't like the sound of that.'

'That's where we going,' said Raven Boy and, with that, they climbed back aboard the magic flying carpet.

'Take us to Terror Town.'

The carpet sped off across the sand once more.

NINETEEN

ven Boy and Elf Girl
ld the record for the
mber of times they've
naged to avoid being
n by trolls. Most people
get eaten first time.

A bright moon hung over their heads as they sped across the desert.

'I'm not exactly keen to get there quickly,' admitted Elf Girl.

'Nor me,' said Raven Boy. 'Finding Terrible Tim, last seen at the Horror Hotel in Terror Town. Not exactly a recipe for fun.'

'At least we have the Tears of the Moon,' said Elf Girl.

Raven Boy nodded.

'But we have to find the sword too,' he
said. 'That's what Mervin the Sandman told us.'

Elf Girl sighed.

Then she screamed.

'Oh, come on, Elf Girl,' said Raven Boy.
'It's not that bad.'

Elf Girl didn't reply, but jumped up and grabbed her bow and pointed it at Raven Boy, who was sitting at the back end of the rug.

'Was it something I said?' he asked. 'Elf Girl?'

'Get down!' Elf Girl shouted. 'And get this rug to speed up!'

Raven Boy did as she said as Elf Girl fired her bow, not at Raven Boy, but over his shoulder. He spun round to see another flying carpet behind them. It was smouldering at the edges slightly, leaving behind a trail of smoke, and on board Raven Boy saw three familiar figures.

'Oh no,' he groaned, 'not them.'

There, on the rug behind them, hard on their heels, were the three trolls, also known as Cedric, Bob and Bert.

'They must have followed us all that way and stolen a burning carpet,' cried Elf Girl, and she fired again.

The bow sent some real arrows hurtling towards them, but at the speeds both carpets were travelling, it was very hard to be accurate.

The trolls' carpet was getting closer by the second, but it ducked and it wove as Elf Girl kept firing.

'Try something else!' suggested Raven Boy.

'I just need one steady shot,' said Elf Girl, letting fly another arrow, which sped away and somehow ended up sticking out of Cedric's bottom.

'Ow!' they heard the big troll cry. 'That really hurts! I'm gonna eat you without cooking you for that!'

He waved his fist and their carpet moved even closer, pulling alongside.

'Elf Girl!' screamed Raven Boy. 'Do something!'

Bob and Bert were making ready to jump across from one carpet to the other, while Cedric was struggling to reach around behind him to pull the arrow out.

'Quickly!' wailed Raven Boy and Elf Girl fired again, this time aiming not at the trolls, but the carpet upon which they were flying.

A jet of fire shot from her bow, and struck the carpet full on. It burned into ash in moments, disappearing, and leaving the trolls hovering in mid-air for a split second before they plummeted down.

The last Elf Girl and Raven Boy saw of them was three sets of legs sticking out of the sand, their feet waving.

'You really do know what you're doing!' Raven Boy shouted and gave Elf Girl a huge hug, and Elf Girl was so happy, she didn't like to tell him that she'd actually been trying to turn it into water.

'We're unbeatable!' cried Raven Boy. 'We can do this! We can really beat the Goblin King. We have the Tears of the Moon, now all we need is the Singing Sword.'

Despite herself, Elf Girl couldn't help cheering up.

'You're right, Raven Boy. We are invincible! Let's go!'

'Onwards to Terror Town!'

'Onwards!'

They shivered, not just because night had fallen, but also because they really, really, didn't want to go there.

They hugged each other and sped on into the night, until, without warning, Shona piped up.

'Ten minutes to landing. Please take your seats. Ten minutes till Terror Town.'

Raven Boy swallowed hard.

Elf Girl looked determined.

Rat squeaked as bravely as he could.

And in ten minutes they were there.

They'd arrived at Terror Town.

NEXT

Follow Raven Boy and Elf Girl (and Rat) as their adventures continue in TERROR TOWN . . .

Fright Forest

Monster Mountains

Scream Sea

Dread Desert

Terror Town

Creepy Caves

the
orion star

Sign up for **the orion star**
newsletter to get inside information
about your favourite children's authors
as well as exclusive competitions and
early reading copy giveaways.

www.orionbooks.co.uk/newsletters

Follow @the_orionstar on .